For Taylor Rose—may your dreams take you far, wherever you are. — J. L. R.

To Isaac. — K. B.

Text copyright © 2021 Judith L. Roth. Illustrations copyright © 2021 Kendra Binney. First published in 2021 by Page Street Kids,

an imprint of Page Street Publishing Co., 27 Congress Street, Suite 105, Salem, MA 01970. www.pagestreetpublishing.com. All rights reserved.

No part of this book may be reproduced or used, in any form or by any means, electronic or mechanical, without prior permission in writing from the publisher.

Distributed by Macmillan, sales in Canada by The Canadian Manda Group. ISBN-13: 978-1-64567-084-1. ISBN-10: 1-64567-084-8.

CIP data for this book is available from the Library of Congress. This book was typeset in Macaron. The illustrations were done in acrylic and watercolor and then digitally collaged.

Cover and book design by Meha Parsloe for Page Street Kids. Printed and bound in Shenzhen, Guangdong, China

20 21 22 23 24 CCO 5 4 3 2 1

Page Street Publishing uses only materials from suppliers who are committed to responsible and sustainable forest management.
Page Street Publishing protects our planet by donating to nonprofits like The Trustees, which focuses on local land conservation.

Venetian Lullaby

Judith L. Roth

illustrated by Kendra Binney

PAGE
STREET
KiDS

Hear the water lap, lap.
Time to take a nap.
Drop the oar in deep, deep.
Time to go to sleep.

Wrap up in this blanket, baby.
Cuddle on my lap.
Rest your eyes while pigeons rise.
Time to take a nap.

Curl up like a drowsy kitty
dozing in the square.
Float like kites of drying laundry
lifting in the air.

Boatman's gonna sing, baby.
Close your sleepy eyes.
Bells are gonna swing and ring.
Music in the skies.

All around the stony city,
lions lift their wings.
Watch them fly through cloud and sky.
Dream of lovely things.

Drift down streets of water, baby.
Close your sleepy eyes.
Dipping oars and curtain doors
sigh their lullabies.

Count the wells and curvy bridges.
Number them like sheep.
Masks in windows, made for dreaming,
ease you soft toward sleep.

Feel the boat a-bobbing, baby.
Close your sleepy eyes.
Past the peace of cobbled streets—
there your dreamland lies.

Neighbors on the bridges babble,
murmur light and low.
Down here in your cradle boat,
let your stirring slow.

Mama's gonna sing, baby.
Close your sleepy eyes.
Time to go to sleep, my angel.
(Hush, you dragonflies.)

Hear the water lap, lap.
Time to take a nap.
Drifting down so deep, deep . . . .

falling . . . . fast . . . . asleep.